mary-kateandashley

TWO of a kind ™

Le~~WITHDRAWN~~

FROM STOCK

by Megan Stine

from the series created by Robert Griffard
& ~~[illegible]~~

D1079816

📚 HarperCollins*Entertainment*
An Imprint of HarperCollinsPublishers

A PARACHUTE PRESS BOOK

A PARACHUTE PRESS BOOK
Parachute Publishing, L.L.C.
156 Fifth Avenue
Suite 325
NEW YORK
NY 10010

First published in the USA by HarperEntertainment 1999
First published in Great Britain by HarperCollins*Entertainment* 2002
HarperCollins*Entertainment* is an imprint of HarperCollins*Publishers* Ltd,
77-85 Fulham Palace Road, Hammersmith, London W6 8JB

TWO OF A KIND, characters, names and all related indicia are trademarks of
Warner Bros.TM & © 1999 American Broadcasting Company, Inc.
TWO OF A KIND books created and produced by Parachute
Publishing, L.L.C., in cooperation with Dualstar Publications,
a division of Dualstar Entertainment Group, Inc..

Cover photograph courtesy of Dualstar Entertainment Group, Inc.
© Dualstar Entertainment Group, Inc. 1998

The HarperCollins website address is
www.fireandwater.com

5 7 9 8 6

The authors assert the moral right to be
identified as the authors of the work.

ISBN 0 00 714473 3

Printed and bound in Great Britain by Clays Ltd, St Ives plc

CHAPTER ONE

"It's totally not fair," Jennifer Dilber complained to Ashley Burke. "So what if my birthday happens to be a week before Christmas? I should still be able to have a party!"

"Absolutely!" Ashley agreed, nodding. "Having a party is just standard! Your parents will have to give in."

Ashley gazed around the dress section at Bailey's, her favourite shop. She, Jennifer, Akilah, and Nicole were all shopping at the mall. They had already been there a whole hour.

"And here's what I'm wearing to your party," Ashley exclaimed. She grabbed a short black dress off the rack. "Isn't it perfect?"

The dress had a flared skirt and spaghetti straps. Ashley held it up for her friends to see.

Jennifer eyed the dress. "Black's not your colour," she said.

"How can it not be my colour?" Ashley argued. "I wear black all the time!"

Jennifer rolled her eyes. "It would look better on me," she grumbled. "Besides, my parents won't give in. There's *no way* I'm having a party. So forget it. You don't have any reason to buy that dress."

"Wow – *you're* in a bad mood," Nicole said.

"Well, excuse me," Jennifer snapped. "Wouldn't you be?"

Nicole shrugged. "I guess."

"I don't blame Jennifer," Ashley said, defending her friend. "I mean, it's horribly unfair that your parents won't let you have a birthday party! A fancy birthday party would be so . . . so . . . ."

"Fabulous," Akilah said, finishing Ashley's sentence. "Can't you just picture it? We'd all get new dresses. The guys would have to wear something nice – no T-shirts or jeans allowed."

"Forget it," Jennifer said. "I begged my parents for an hour last night. All they said was, 'Not this year.' They wouldn't even think about it. I'm positive they won't change their minds." She sighed. "This is going to be the most miserable birthday ever."

Poor Jennifer, Ashley thought. She wished there was a way to cheer her friend up, but she knew it was hopeless. Unless . . .

Unless she gave Jennifer a surprise party! Yes!

She would give Jennifer the most fantastic surprise party in the whole world!

It would be just like Akilah said. Fabulous. The house would be all decorated for Christmas, and everything would look beautiful. They'd have a Christmas tree and candles everywhere. And she'd invite the cutest guys from school.

Plus, Ashley would have the perfect excuse to get a new dress. Bonus!

"What are *you* looking so happy about?" Jennifer asked.

Whoops! Ashley wiped the smile off her face.

"I'm not happy," she said, covering up quickly. "I was just thinking about what we could do on your birthday . . . uh, instead of a party. Like maybe you could all come over and spend the night. We'll rent three videos. Order pizza. Stay up all night."

"Maybe," Jennifer answered glumly.

"You see, everything will be great," Ashley told her. She glanced at her watch. "But we're late! We were supposed to meet Carrie at the fountain down at the lower level five minutes ago."

Ashley led the way as the four girls zipped through the crowds to meet Carrie. When they neared the fountain, Ashley spotted her sitting on the bench.

Carrie Moore was Ashley's babysitter. She was in one of the science classes Ashley's father, Kevin Burke, taught at the local college. He had hired Carrie to take care of Ashley and her twin sister Mary-Kate. Ever since the twins' mother died three years ago, they needed someone to be home with them after school. Carrie was the coolest babysitter they'd ever had. And the best thing was, last month she'd moved into the house! She always let Mary-Kate and Ashley hang out in the great apartment she fixed up for herself in their basement.

"Sorry we're late," Ashley said as she and her friends rushed up to meet Carrie.

"You're not late," Carrie answered. "You're right on time."

"But you said to meet you at three – and it's ten past," Akilah said. "So, aren't we ten minutes late?"

"Nope." Carrie shook her head. "Everyone knows how hard it is to stop shopping. When you're shopping, ten minutes late is right on time.

4

So, do you think you're ready to go?"

"Not yet," Jennifer blurted out.

Ashley glanced at her friend. Jennifer looked almost happy for the first time that day. She was staring at someone across the mall.

Quickly Jennifer started fixing her long blonde hair. She brushed it back so it draped smoothly on her shoulders.

"Who are you staring at?" Ashley asked.

"It's him," Jennifer whispered. "Parker Branford. The guy I told you about."

Ashley followed Jennifer's stare.

Yup. There he was. The gorgeous, ninth-grade boy Jennifer had a crush on. The one who didn't even know Jennifer was alive.

How could he? Ashley thought. *Ninth-grade boys never notice seventh-grade girls.*

Parker was wandering through the mall with another ninth grader, Trevor Domingo.

"He is so cute!" Jennifer exclaimed.

"Trevor isn't bad, either," Nicole said softly.

"That's what I want for my birthday," Jennifer decided. "Parker. Just dress him up, and stick a bow on his head, and I don't care if I never have another party!"

"Parker Branford?" Akilah said. "Dream on."

"Can we stay a little longer?" Jennifer begged Carrie. Her eyes were locked on Parker as he and Trevor made their way through the mall.

"I don't know." Carrie shrugged her shoulders. "I mean, are you thinking of following them?"

Jennifer blushed and nodded.

"Because it looks to me like they're following those three high-school girls," Carrie pointed out. "So this could get ugly. You don't want it to turn into a parade!"

Jennifer craned her neck. Ashley did, too.

Carrie was right. Parker and Trevor were trailing three older girls – one redhead and two brunettes. They all slipped into a music shop.

"Oh, well." Jennifer gave a long, loud sigh. "See? I told you this was going to be a lousy birthday."

"Your birthday isn't for two weeks," Nicole reminded her. "Aren't you sulking a little early?"

"It's never too early to sulk," Jennifer replied. "Maybe my parents will start feeling guilty. At least then they'll buy me more presents!"

Two weeks, Ashley thought. *That's just enough time to plan the party.* She could hardly wait to get home and ask her dad for permission.

He just has to say yes, she decided. *He has no choice!* She thought about the party all the way home in the car. She made up a guest list. Planned the decorations. And thought about the new dress she'd get to buy!

But she couldn't say a word to Nicole or Akilah. Not with Jennifer right there. Nicole was dropped off first. Then Akilah. Jennifer's house was last.

"See you in school on Monday," Ashley called.

Finally Carrie pulled up to the Burkes' house.

Ashley jumped out of the car and ran towards the front door. She almost bumped into Mary-Kate's friend Amanda Bennett, who was on her way out.

"Whoops! Sorry," Ashley said.

"No problem. I get rammed a lot worse in soccer practice," Amanda said. She gave Ashley a little wave, then stepped around her and trotted down the front path.

Ashley burst into the house and headed straight for her dad. He was sitting on the couch, watching a basketball game with Mary-Kate.

"Hi, Dad," she said. "Hey, Mary-Kate. Dad, I need to ask you something really important." She turned the sound down on the TV. "Can I have a surprise party for Jennifer's birthday?"

"When?" Kevin Burke asked.

"Two weeks from today," Ashley answered.

Kevin thought for a moment, then shook his

head. "I'm sorry, Ashley," he answered. "We can't have two parties here on the same night."

"Two parties!" Ashley yelped. "What do you mean – two parties? Who's giving the other one?"

Mary-Kate turned and looked at her. "That would be me," she said.

CHAPTER TWO

"*You're* giving a party?" Ashley's mouth dropped open. She stared at her sister. "Since when?"

"I just decided today," Mary-Kate explained. "Dad said it was okay. It's a surprise party for Amanda. Her birthday is that week."

"But you can't!" Ashley exclaimed. "I mean, I have this all planned!"

"Calm down, Ashley." Kevin turned off the TV. "Why can't you choose another night?"

"Yeah," Mary-Kate said. "I'll go get the calendar off the fridge."

Mary-Kate trotted into the kitchen, then back to the living room. She and Ashley crowded on to the sofa with their dad. Carrie leaned over their shoulders. All

9

four of them studied the rows of boxes.

"I can't have Jennifer's party on a school night, and everything else is taken," Ashley complained.

Mary-Kate double-checked. Ashley was right. Every weekend night for the next two weekends was booked. And then it was Christmas.

"Maybe you can have one big party – together," Kevin suggested.

Ashley looked at Mary-Kate. "Maybe. Here's what I was thinking. We get everyone to dress up, we put on some great music for dancing, we serve Sprite in fancy glasses. It will be so—"

"So *not* Amanda," Mary-Kate interrupted. She was sure Amanda would hate the kind of party Ashley was describing. Mary-Kate and Amanda were a lot alike – both of them liked softball, basketball, and butterscotch sundaes. And both of them were jeans and-T-shirt types.

"Besides, if we get all dressed up, how are we supposed to play Twister, Ping-Pong and air hockey?" Mary-Kate demanded.

Ashley screwed up her face. "Twister?" she said. "Whose idea is that?"

"Mine," Mary-Kate answered. "And video games. And pin the tail on the Chicago Bulls – just for kicks. It's so goofy, Amanda will love it."

Ashley shook her head. "Jennifer would faint if anyone played those – those *babyish* games at her birthday party," she said. "Her party has to be sophisticated and elegant. I've got it all planned."

"You've got it all planned for next year," Mary-Kate said. "Because we're not doing any of that stuff this year. Not at Amanda's party."

"Dad?" Ashley pleaded. "Help!"

"Dad, I can't invite Amanda over for a night of birthday torture," Mary-Kate protested. "And that's what Ashley's party would be. Total torture!"

Kevin shook his head. "You girls have to work it out," he said. "Mary-Kate has first dibs on the house, so it's up to her. Whatever she agrees to is fine with me."

"Thank you," Mary-Kate said with a nod.

Ashley turned to her sister. "Please, Mary-Kate," she begged. "Jennifer is turning thirteen – and her parents won't even let her have a party!"

"I wish I could help you out," Mary-Kate answered. "But it's Amanda's birthday, too. And I don't see how we can have a party that she and Jennifer will both like."

Carrie spoke up for the first time. "What if . . . "

"What if what?" Ashley asked eagerly. "You have an idea?"

Carrie nodded. "Maybe we could have two parties on the same night. Ashley, you could have your fancy dance upstairs, in the living room. And Mary-Kate – you could have your bash downstairs in my apartment!"

"Really?" Ashley asked. Her eyes lit up.

Not a bad idea, Mary-Kate thought. The basement was the best place to play Twister and air hockey.

"Okay, it's a deal," Mary-Kate told Ashley.

"Thank you!" Ashley screamed. She leaned over and gave her sister a hug. "Now I can get a new dress!"

Mary-Kate laughed. "All I have to do is make sure my favourite jeans are clean. But I'll make you a bet," she added.

"What's that?" Ashley asked.

"I'll bet my party is a lot more fun than yours," Mary-Kate declared.

"Oh, right." Ashley rolled her eyes. "Twister and pin the tail? Can't wait. If things get really rocking, you can always play hide-and-seek."

"Just you wait and see," Mary-Kate said. "My friends are going to have an awesome time."

Ashley shrugged. "Whatever. You do your thing, Mary-Kate. And I'll do mine. And may the best party win!"

CHAPTER THREE

"Carrie – help!" Mary-Kate moaned.

She clicked the mouse on her computer five times. Nothing happened. The screen was frozen. Mary-Kate threw up her hands in frustration.

"You're asking *me* for help on the computer?" Carrie replied. "Isn't that like asking the captain of the *Titanic* for tips on icebergs?"

Mary-Kate laughed. "Yeah, I guess it is," she admitted. "But *someone's* got to help me make this software work."

"What are you doing?" Carrie strolled towards the table where Mary-Kate was working.

"I'm designing my own invitations for Amanda's surprise party," Mary-Kate explained. "And they've got to be great. I'm sending them by e-mail."

"That's so cool," Carrie said. "But do all your friends have e-mail?"

Mary-Kate checked her guest list. "All but three," she reported. "So for those, I'll print out copies of the invitation and give out them at school."

"Sounds good. What's the problem?" Carrie asked.

"This programme isn't working," Mary-Kate complained. "I'm trying to put in these little pictures – a soccer ball, a pizza, and a video game. But every time I click on them they disappear."

Carrie glanced over Mary-Kate's shoulder. On the screen was a colourful page of type. It said:

Please Come to

A SURPRISE BIRTHDAY PARTY!

When: Saturday, December 16 at 7:00

Where: Mary-Kate's house

What: Ping Pong, Twister, video games,

Tons of food!

Don't forget: Dress casual.

And keep the secret!

"It looks great, Mary-Kate!" Carrie said. "I love all those different kinds of type."

"Thanks." Mary-Kate beamed. "But what about the clip art?"

Carrie shrugged. "Paul is on his way over now. Maybe he can help."

"Perfect!" Mary-Kate exclaimed.

Paul was in Kevin Burke's science class with Carrie. He was kind of nerdy, but he was a computer whiz. He'd be able to fix Mary-Kate's software in a microsecond.

While she waited for Paul to arrive, Mary-Kate wrote an e-mail to Amanda's parents. She told them all about the surprise party. Her letter spelled out the date, the time, everything.

"Please make sure Amanda is home that night," Mary-Kate wrote. "I'm going to call her up at the last minute and invite her for a sleepover. That way she'll never suspect a thing!"

When the message was finished, Mary-Kate clicked on the send button.

A minute later Paul walked in the door. He took one look at the computer screen and knew what was wrong. Two minutes later, he was clicking the mouse – and all the little pictures fell into place.

"You're a genius!" Mary-Kate declared.

"Tell that to your dad," Paul answered. "He hasn't given me my final grade yet."

"I'll tell him you deserve an A in clip art, for sure," Mary-Kate joked. Then she got to work sending out the e-mail invitations.

Ashley came bouncing down the stairs. "Carrie, do we have any pretty postage stamps?" she asked.

Mary-Kate glanced up. Ashley had a thick stack of envelopes in her hand.

Those must be her party invitations, Mary-Kate thought. *They look really fancy.*

"In the kitchen," Carrie answered.

Ashley dropped the stack of envelopes on the table and hurried to get the stamps.

Ashley had used a calligraphy pen to address the envelopes, and her handwriting looked like art, with big loops and curls.

Since they weren't sealed yet, Mary-Kate picked one up. She took the invitation out and stared at it.

"Wow," she muttered under her breath.

It was the fanciest party invitation she'd ever seen! The paper was thick, with a gold rim. Pink and green flowers decorated the border.

In the middle the party information looked as if it was printed in black ink. But Mary-Kate knew Ashley had used the laser printer. The type read:

You are Invited to

*A Winter Wonderland
Surprise Birthday Party*

**For Jennifer
December 16, 7:00 P.M.
At Ashley Burke's House
Music, Dancing, Fine Food
Semi-formal Dress
(No Jeans or T-shirts, Please)**

Mary-Kate stared at the invitations. *Who does Ashley think she's inviting?* she wondered. *The Queen of England?*

Mary-Kate felt her throat tighten up a little. Ashley's invitations were awesome. Okay, maybe they were a little overdone for Mary-Kate's taste. *But a lot of girls will really like them,* she thought.

"Aren't they great?" Ashley said when she returned from the kitchen.

"Uh, yeah," Mary-Kate admitted. "They're nice. But what's up with this 'fine food' part? What are you serving? Nachos with caviar?"

Ashley looked horrified.

"Crisps are so . . . so yesterday," she replied,

tossing her hair over her shoulders. "We're having only the most elegant foods at my party."

"Do the guys on your guest list know that?" Mary-Kate asked. "Because I bet they won't be too excited about asparagus on slices of pumpernickel. Or whatever."

"For one thing, I'm serving chocolate-covered strawberries," Ashley answered. "And for another, I happen to know that they're Michael Barnstein's favourite food."

"You're inviting Michael Barnstein?" Mary-Kate's mouth dropped open in shock. "But he's one of Amanda's best friends!"

"So?" Ashley shrugged. "Akilah has a crush on him. I had to invite him to my party."

Mary-Kate grabbed the stack of envelopes and flipped through them. Her eyes grew wider.

"Ashley!" she complained. "You invited Brian and Max! And Michelle, Carly, and Rebecca! That's half the people on my guest list!"

"What's wrong with that?" Ashley said.

"They're Amanda's friends," Mary-Kate argued. "Now they'll have to choose which party to come to."

"So let them choose," Ashley said simply. "What's wrong with that?"

Nothing's wrong with it, Mary-Kate thought.

Unless everyone picks your party instead of mine!

"We could have had one big party," Ashley said. "*You* were the one who wanted to make it a competition, don't forget. It was *your* idea – not mine."

Mary-Kate watched Ashley put the pretty flowered stamps on her envelopes. They matched the colour of the calligraphy ink.

Oh, well, Mary-Kate thought with a gulp. *So some people might like Ashley's invitations better than mine. That doesn't mean that they'll decide to go to Ashley's party instead. Does it?*

"Hey, Mary-Kate, thanks for the party invitation," Michael Barnstein said when he met Mary-Kate and Ashley outside school the next morning. They stomped their feet to get the snow off their boots and headed inside.

Mary-Kate glanced around the hallway quickly to make sure Amanda wasn't around. The coast was clear.

"Can you come?" Mary-Kate asked, her voice soft.

"Defini—" Michael began.

"Oh, don't say yes yet," Ashley cried. She lowered her voice to a whisper. "You'll be getting an invitation from me, too. I'm having a surprise birthday party for Jennifer on the same night."

"Oh." Michael looked confused. "Two parties? On the same night?"

"I know Amanda would really want—" Mary-Kate began.

"You don't have to decide right now," Ashley interrupted. "At least wait until you get my invitation, too."

Michael nodded a couple times, shifting from foot to foot. "Yeah, I guess that makes sense. I'll let you, um, both of you, know later. See you." He hurried down the hall to his locker.

"We're having chocolate-covered strawberries at mine," Ashley called after him.

Mary-Kate shot her sister an annoyed look. Michael was about to say he'd come to Amanda's party before Ashley butted in!

"Come on, Mary-Kate." Ashley stared at her upset sister. "I had to tell him about the party for Jennifer. Wouldn't you have told him about Amanda's party if he'd got my invitation first?"

Mary-Kate hesitated for a second. "Yeah," she admitted.

"So you won't mind if I tell a few other people that my invitation is on the way." Ashley darted off before Mary-Kate could answer.

Oh, no! She'll tell everyone about her fancy chocolate-covered strawberries and her fancy decorations and her

20

fancy everything else, Mary-Kate thought. *I've got to do something – quick!*

She raced over to Michael's locker. She was completely willing to let the best party win. But Michael needed a little more information before he decided which party was going to be the *best* party.

"Hey, Michael, I guess you'll be hitting the mall after school," she said casually.

"Huh?" He shoved his jacket into his locker and slammed the door.

"Oh, I just figured that you'd want to get a new tie or something . . . if you decide to go to Ashley's party. You know it's formal, right? No T-shirts or jeans."

"No jeans?" Michael yelped.

"Nope," Mary-Kate answered.

"Put me down for your party," he said.

"Cool!" Mary-Kate answered.

Out of the corner of her eye, she saw Ashley walking away from their friend Max. She said a quick goodbye to Michael.

"Did you get my e-mail?" she said, running up to Max.

"Yup," he said. "But I can't tell you if I'm coming yet. Ashley told me I'll be getting an invitation from her, too. And she promised that at *her* party there'll be lots of babes in short dresses."

Max looked at her as if he was waiting for her to come up with something better.

"We're going to have pizza from Marino's at my party," Mary-Kate said. "Anchovy and broccoli pizza," she added quickly. She tried not to grimace. She knew Max loved the combo, but Mary-Kate thought it was disgusting.

"Anchovy and broccoli. Babes in short dresses," Max muttered to himself.

The bell rang.

"I have to think this over," he told Mary-Kate.

I have one definite yes, Mary-Kate thought as she headed to class. *And one definite maybe.*

She turned the corner and saw Ashley walking down the hall with Carly. Carly was whispering in Ashley's ear. *What is Carly saying?* Mary-Kate wondered. *Is she saying she'll go to Ashley's party?*

Carly was in Mary-Kate's second-period class. Mary-Kate decided that she could talk to her then. And during gym she'd tell Michelle and Rebecca all about her party. Then at lunch she'd have to make sure to sit next to Brian so she could fill him in.

By the end of the day, Mary-Kate would make sure that everyone she knew would be coming to the party – *her* party!

CHAPTER
FOUR

Ashley leaned back on Jennifer's bed and took a long drink of soda. The inside of her mouth felt as dry as a desert. She figured it was from all the extra talking she'd done at school that week.

She'd told every person on her list about how great the party for Jennifer was going to be. But now it was the weekend, and she'd only got two definite yeses.

Ashley promised herself she'd talk to all the maybes again on Monday. Just the thought made her thirsty again. She drained her glass and chomped on one of the ice cubes.

"How do you think I should end this letter?" Jennifer asked from her seat in front of her desk.

"'With my everlasting devotion'? or 'Love until death'?"

"'Love until death'?" Ashley jumped off the bed and hurried to look over Jennifer's shoulder. "What are you writing?"

"A note to Parker Branford," Jennifer answered. "I'm going to throw myself at him and see if *that* works. Because so far, he isn't falling for the cold-shoulder treatment."

"No way! I'm not letting you," Ashley said. She grabbed the note and crumpled it up.

"Hey!" Jennifer complained. "I spent a lot of time on that!"

"Too bad," Ashley declared. "In the name of friendship, I'm saving you from yourself."

She jammed the note in her backpack. She didn't want Jennifer to be able to dig it out of the trash later.

"But I've got to do something," Jennifer moaned. "It's torture just being around him every day. His locker is only two away from mine."

"And he hasn't noticed you yet?" Ashley asked.

Jennifer shook her head. She left her desk and plopped down on the floor next to Ashley. "I guess I should give up," Jennifer sighed. "No boyfriend and no birthday party. I just don't get it." She turned to Ashley. "I don't know why my parents haven't let me have a party."

"Well, hey," Ashley said. "We'll make the best of it. You'll come over to my house on your birthday, and we'll celebrate big time. Videos. Popcorn. And we'll come up with the perfect plan for you to get Parker's attention!"

"Oh, wow. It will be my best birthday ever," Jennifer mumbled.

Ashley frowned. She didn't know what to say to cheer Jennifer up – so she didn't say anything.

The silence stretched out between them.

"Okay, okay." Jennifer finally said. "I'm sorry. You're being a great friend. I'm just mad at my mom and dad. They don't even seem to care how I feel."

That had to hurt big-time, Ashley thought.

"Don't worry," Ashley said. "We'll have a birthday bash that you'll never forget."

"Ashley, does this look like a bull's tail to you?" Mary-Kate asked when Ashley got home from Jennifer's.

Ashley sat across from her at the kitchen table. She studied the piece of construction paper in Mary-Kate's hand. "Yeah, it looks pretty good," she admitted. "But maybe you could put some yarn on it for fur or something."

"Great idea!" Mary-Kate sprang to her feet. "I'm going to go see if Carrie has any." She bolted for the door, then turned back to Ashley. "Hey, thanks for helping out the enemy," she joked.

"No problem," Ashley murmured. She turned the big sheet of drawing paper around to face her and checked out the bull Mary-Kate had drawn. It was cartoony and cute.

She picked up one of the tails, closed her eyes, and tried to jam the tail in place.

When she opened her eyes, she couldn't help smiling. A perfect bull's-eye. Make that bull's-tail. She hadn't lost her touch. She'd always ruled at pin the tail.

She tried to remember the last time she'd played. *It must have been years ago*, Ashley thought. *It would almost be fun to . . .*

Ashley's eyebrows scrunched together. It was way too easy to imagine everyone at Mary-Kate's party cracking up as someone stuck a tail on a lamp or something. Just goofing around.

But it would only be fun for about two seconds, she told herself. *Then everybody would be totally bored.*

Probably.

But probably wasn't good enough. Ashley had

promised Jennifer an unforgettable celebration, and now the party was only a week away. What could she do to make sure everyone had a great time – at *her* party?

Mary-Kate hurried back into the kitchen before Ashley could come up with an answer. "Carrie said I could unravel this old sweater of hers and use the yarn," she announced. She held up a ratty old black cardigan.

Ashley nodded. She was still trying to think up ways to make her party the best ever.

Unfortunately, her mind was totally blank.

She grabbed her backpack off the floor. She figured she should start on her homework. She reached for her history book and felt a crumpled piece of paper. Jennifer's letter to Parker Branford.

Ashley shook her head. Jennifer was totally crazy about the guy.

A tiny smile tugged at her lips as an idea began to form. All Ashley had to do was get Parker Branford to come to the party. Jennifer would be ecstatic. And so would every girl on Ashley's party list. None of them would be able to resist the chance to hang out with one of the cutest guys in the ninth grade.

Ashley's smile grew bigger. And if a ninth-grade guy was going to the party, that would convince all the seventh-grade guys that it was the place to be.

"What are you grinning about?" Mary-Kate asked. She snipped off some yarn from the bottom of Carrie's sweater.

"Nothing," Ashley answered.

Parker Branford was her secret weapon. With an emphasis on secret.

Now all Ashley had to do was figure out how to get him to her party.

She gulped.

Yeah, all she had to do was figure out how to get the most popular boy in the ninth grade to come to a party with a bunch of seventh graders.

How hard could that be?

CHAPTER FIVE

"You really think Parker will come?" Carly's voice rose higher with each word.

Ashley smiled at her in the mirror of the girl's bathroom. "Absolutely," she answered. "I'm going to ask him right now."

"Jennifer is going to freak out," Akilah said as she adjusted the little butterfly clip in her hair.

"Forget Jennifer. *I'm* going to freak out," Michelle declared.

Ashley laughed. Carly and Michelle were both maybes. But it sounded like they were on their way to becoming yeses.

"Maybe Parker will even bring a couple of his friends. What do you think?" Carly asked. Her voice still didn't sound quite normal.

"Sure. He might," Ashley answered. She pulled her lip gloss out of her purse and applied a fresh coat.

"Can I borrow that?" Akilah asked. "I love the colour."

"Sure," Ashley said. She handed the lip gloss over. She studied her reflection for a long moment. Lip gloss. Check. Hair. Check. Lucky necklace. Check.

"Time to do it," she whispered. If she waited much longer, lunch would be over, and she'd miss Parker. They didn't have any classes together.

"I'm out of here," she told the others. She hoped they didn't notice the small quiver in her voice. She didn't want them to think she couldn't get Parker.

Even if she wasn't so sure herself.

"See you in English," Akilah called after her.

Ashley took a deep breath as she stepped into the hall and headed down to the cafeteria. It felt as if the shake in her voice had travelled down to her knees.

"Parker Branford is just a guy," Ashley muttered. "You talk to guys all the time. You have friends who are guys. Just get over it."

"Ashley, if you're going to talk to yourself, can't you wait until you get home?"

Ashley turned to see Mary-Kate. She was

standing with Rebecca by Rebecca's locker.

"Oh, uh, I didn't realise I was," she answered, feeling her face get hot. "I was just, uh, practising for that oral report I have to give next week."

Ashley hurried by them and continued to the cafeteria. She took another deep breath, then shoved through the double doors. She scanned the large room for Parker.

She didn't see him.

He has to be here, she thought. *He has to be.*

She checked the cafeteria again, forcing herself to look at each person.

Yes! There he was, over by the soda machine. He was facing away from her, but Ashley recognised him by the way his hair curled over his collar. Jennifer was always raving about those curls.

Ashley didn't give herself time to get even more nervous. She headed straight over to Parker and flashed him a big smile.

"Hi," she said.

Not a brilliant opening. But at least her voice didn't squeak or anything. And she was pretty sure he couldn't see her knees shaking.

He looked down at her as if she were a mildly interesting bug.

"Hi," he answered.

"Uh, I'm having a surprise birthday party for Jennifer Dilber next Saturday. And, uh, I was wondering if you'd like to come?"

Parker popped open the top of his soda and took a swig. Then he glanced down at her again.

"When is it?" he asked.

"Next Saturday," Ashley repeated. "At seven o'clock."

She nibbled off a little of her lip gloss. The fake strawberry flavour tasted sour on her tongue.

Why can't he just say he'll be there? she thought.

"It's going to be great. There's going to be lots of dancing," she added.

Ashley saw that Parker wasn't even looking at her. He was staring right over the top of her head.

"There's going to be tons of great food, too," she said in a rush. "Chocolate-covered strawberries and little pastries. I got the recipe for the pastry from a cookbook. It's made with real cream."

Stop! Stop now! Ashley begged herself. *You sound like a total idiot.*

She shook her hair off her face and gave Parker another smile. "So, can you come?"

"Hey, Parker, are you going to stand there talking to your girlfriend, or are you coming?" someone shouted from a table by the window.

"Sorry, I'm busy that night," Parker said quickly. He turned away from her.

"Well, if you change your mind . . ." Ashley let her words trail off. It was obvious Parker wasn't listening any more.

"Oh!" She took two steps forward and grabbed him by his sleeve.

He looked down at her hand as if he couldn't believe what he was seeing. Ashley snatched it away.

"I just wanted to say, please don't say anything to Jennifer. The party's a surprise."

Parker started to back away. "I won't say anything to . . . what was her name again?"

"Jennifer." Ashley's throat felt tight.

"Right. Jennifer. Anyway, see you," Parker said. And he was gone.

Wow, Ashley thought. *I've been rejected before. But it feels a lot worse being rejected by a ninth-grade boy!*

She wanted to slink away.

But she couldn't. Akilah, Carly and Michelle were standing in the back of the cafeteria. They all had their eyes locked on Ashley.

She lifted her chin and walked towards them with what she hoped was a happy expression on her face.

"Well?" Carly asked.

"Well?" Michelle repeated. She gave a little bounce on her toes.

"Well . . ." Ashley hesitated for a second. "Well, Parker thinks the party sounds really cool," she answered.

Carly let out a little squeal. Michelle gave a double bounce.

"If Parker's there, then I'm there!" Carly declared.

"Me too," Michelle agreed.

Ashley started to feel a little queasy.

What I told them wasn't totally a lie, Ashley reassured herself.

Not really.

Parker didn't say what he thought about the party one way *or* the other.

And, anyway, it didn't matter. Ashley was still going to find a way to make sure Parker showed up. No matter what it took!

CHAPTER SIX

"Ashley, want to try some of this cheddar cheese popcorn?" Mary-Kate asked as she sat down on the arm of the sofa. "Carrie showed me how to make it. I'm thinking of having it at my party."

Ashley didn't answer.

Mary-Kate shook the bowl of popcorn under her sister's nose. "Come on. I promise I won't tell anyone at school that you eat ordinary food," she joked.

"No, thanks. I'm just not hungry," Ashley answered.

"Are you okay?" Mary-Kate asked.

"Mary-Kate, telephone," Carrie called from the kitchen.

Maybe it's someone calling to say they're coming to my party! Mary-Kate thought. She jumped up and raced to the phone.

"Hello?" she said.

"Hi, it's Max. I just wanted to say that I decided I'm going to go to Ashley's party," he said without pausing to take a breath. "See you in school, okay?"

Mary-Kate heard a click. Then the dial tone.

She slowly hung up the phone. As soon as she did, it rang again.

"Hello?" Mary-Kate said.

Please let it be Max saying he was only kidding, she thought.

"I know I said I'd go to your party," a new voice said. "But I, um, I decided that . . . uh, I, I really like chocolate-covered strawberries. And it's not going to kill me to get dressed up, I guess."

"Wait. Who is this?" Mary-Kate asked. Just then she heard a beeping noise. Someone else was trying to get through.

"Just a second. Don't go away," she said to the voice on the other end of the line. She pressed the Call Waiting button.

"Hello," she said.

"Oh, hi, Mary-Kate?" It was Amanda. "I haven't seen you all day. I wanted to ask you about our social studies homework. I'm sort of confused. Do you think Mrs. Ramirez wants us to—"

Mary-Kate cut Amanda off. "Listen, I can't talk now," she said rapidly. "Call-you-later-bye . . ."

She pressed the Call Waiting button again. "Are you still there?" she said.

"Oh, yeah. It's me, Michael," the voice answered. "I have to go. I have to, um, take the dog for a walk."

He hung up almost as fast as Max had.

Mary-Kate wandered back into the living room. She sat down next to Ashley and threw some popcorn into her mouth.

After she swallowed it, she realised she was so upset that she had no idea what it tasted like.

She picked up the remote and clicked on the TV. "Anything you want to watch?" she asked Ashley.

"I don't care," Ashley answered.

Mary-Kate noticed that Ashley had a tiny little line over her nose. The one she always got when she was thinking hard.

"What's up with—" Mary-Kate began.

The phone rang again.

Don't let it be for me! Mary-Kate thought.

But a second later Carrie was calling her to the phone again. "You're popular today," she said as

Mary-Kate stepped back into the kitchen.

"Yeah, right," Mary-Kate muttered. She took the phone from Carrie. "Hello?" she said.

"Hey, it's Brian. I was calling to say your party sounds great."

Mary-Kate let out a breath. "Then you're coming?" she exclaimed. "Awesome! It's going to be tons of fun. We're—"

"Wait. Hold on," Brian interrupted. "You didn't let me finish. Your party sounds great, but I'm going to go to Ashley's. Why are you giving parties on the same night, anyway?"

"Well, it seemed like a good idea at the time," Mary-Kate mumbled.

The next day Mary-Kate gave herself a little pep talk as she went through the cafeteria line.

Okay, she told herself. *Michael said he was going to go to your party. Then he changed his mind. If he changed his mind once, he can change it again. And so can Max and Brian.*

But before she could figure out *how* to get them to change their minds, she needed to know why they'd chosen Ashley's party in the first place.

Mary-Kate paid the cashier, then headed over to her usual table. Rebecca and Carly were the first ones there.

"Hi," they said in unison as Mary-Kate took the seat across from them.

"Can I ask you guys something?" Mary-Kate glanced over her shoulder at the cafeteria line. Amanda was standing on the hot food line, so they had a few minutes to talk before she sat down.

"What's up?" Rebecca asked.

"Yesterday Michael, Max, and Brian all told me they're not coming to my surprise party for Amanda. They're going to Ashley's party instead. I wondered—" Mary-Kate hesitated, then rushed on. "I wondered if you had any idea why."

Rebecca looked at Carly. Carly looked at Rebecca. There was silence.

Rebecca finally spoke up. "Well, I guess it's the Parker Branford thing."

"Huh?" Mary-Kate didn't get it.

"Since Parker Branford is going to Ashley's party, all the guys are thinking it's the cool place to be," Rebecca said.

"And it doesn't hurt that a ton of girls are going to Ashley's party now that Parker's going, either," Carly added with a giggle. "The guys want to be where the girls are!"

"But all the girls *aren't* going to Ashley's party,"

Mary-Kate protested.

Rebecca looked uncomfortable. "Well, I know Michelle is. Plus Akilah and Nicole," she said.

"You're both coming to mine though, right?" Mary-Kate asked.

"Definitely," Rebecca answered.

Carly pulled the paper wrapping off her straw and folded it into a tiny square. "My mom said I could get a new dress if I go to Ashley's party," she admitted. She stared down at her hamburger as if she was talking to it instead of to Mary-Kate. "There's this one I've been wanting forever, and now—"

"Shh!" Rebecca hissed. "Amanda's coming."

"How come everyone stopped talking the minute I arrived?" Amanda asked as she sat down next to Mary-Kate.

"We didn't," Carly said.

Mary-Kate could tell Amanda didn't believe her. She looked a little mad.

"Mary-Kate, you didn't call me back last night," Amanda complained. "I had to call Max about the homework."

"Oh, uh, sorry," Mary-Kate said. She was so worried about her party, she'd forgotten all about Amanda. She stole a glance at her friend. Amanda had a frown on her face.

Amanda would understand soon, Mary-Kate thought. As soon as she walked into the basement and heard everyone yelling, "Surprise!"

That is, if there *was* an everyone.

Mary-Kate gave herself another pep talk.

Okay, everyone wants to go to Ashley's party because Parker Branford is going to be there, she told herself. *So all you need to do is get someone better than Parker to come to yours.*

But who?

"Oh, no!" Amanda cried, jerking Mary-Kate out of her thoughts.

"What?" Mary-Kate exclaimed.

"I just got mustard all over Toni Kukoc!" Amanda grabbed a napkin and scrubbed the yellow splotch on her Chicago Bulls T-shirt. "It's not coming out!" she wailed.

"You can still see all the other players," Sarah said.

Amanda grabbed a second napkin and kept on rubbing. "Toni's my favourite. I don't even want this shirt any more if you can't see *him*!"

That answers my question, Mary-Kate thought. *I'm inviting Toni Kukoc to Amanda's party.*

A real Chicago Bull is much better than Parker Branford any day!

CHAPTER SEVEN

"It's perfect!" Mary-Kate explained to Carrie. "Amanda will love having Toni Kukoc at her party. The guys will love it. And once the girls find out most of the guys will be at my party, they'll be there, too. Parker Branford or no Parker Branford."

"It makes sense," Carrie said slowly. She stuck cotton balls between her toes and unscrewed a bottle of blue nail polish. "But I don't know, Mary-Kate. Toni Kukoc's a star. I really don't think he'd come to a birthday party."

"I remember Amanda telling me he went to a fan's wedding once," Mary-Kate told her. "So why would Kukoc say no to me?"

"Kukoc must have already known the fan or

something," Carrie argued. "Celebrities don't usually do that sort of thing."

"But, Carrie, I have to at least ask him," Mary-Kate said. She felt desperate. "I don't know what else to do. It's my last chance."

Carrie gazed at her sympathetically. "Okay," she said. "I guess it doesn't hurt to try. But if you send an invitation to him care of the team, he'll never get it in time. Your party's only a few days away."

"I know," Mary-Kate answered. "But I've got that all figured out. I'm going to buy a ticket to Friday night's game, and then wait for him to—"

"The game's sold out," Carrie interrupted.

"What?" Mary-Kate shrieked. "Are you kidding?"

"Nope," Carrie said, shaking her head. "But – I happen to have two tickets! Want to go with me?"

"Yes!" Mary-Kate cheered. She reached over and gave Carrie a big hug. "Oops. Sorry," she said when Carrie painted nail polish up her foot.

"Don't worry about it." Carrie grabbed another cotton ball and wiped off the polish. "Mind you, I still don't think we'll even get to talk to Kukoc. And I have to warn you, we're not going to be in the best seats."

"Um – how high are they?" Mary-Kate asked.

Carrie raised an eyebrow. "Let's just say I have a

feeling there won't be anyone sitting behind us."

"I don't care. You have saved my party," Mary-Kate said. "I'm going to make this the happiest day of Amanda's life!"

"Mary-Kate! Wait!" Amanda called after school the next day.

Mary-Kate turned around so fast, she almost slipped on the icy pavement.

Amanda hurried up to her, and they continued down the walkway together. "Remember me?" she said in a grumpy tone. "You were supposed to call me last night! So we could talk about Friday."

Oh, no! Mary-Kate was so busy planning her party for Saturday that she forgot all about Amanda. Again.

Mary-Kate's mind raced to make up an excuse. "Uh, wow, what a night!" she stammered. "All that homework! I've been doing nothing but cramming."

Amanda raised her eyebrows. "Homework? You?" she asked.

"Uh, yeah," Mary-Kate said, quickly. "I guess the holiday spirit is just making me homework crazy or something."

That makes no sense, Mary-Kate thought.

"Well, are you doing homework Friday night?"

Amanda asked. "Or can you come over and watch a movie like we planned?"

Mary-Kate had forgotten all that, too.

"Oh, no, I'm so sorry," Mary-Kate moaned. "I, uh, promised Carrie I'd go out with her on Friday."

Amanda stopped walking and just stood there in the cold. "You're dumping me to go out with your *babysitter*?" she demanded.

All Mary-Kate could do was nod.

"Where are you going?" Amanda asked.

"To a Bulls game," Mary-Kate admitted. Amanda didn't answer, but she did start walking again. Mary-Kate trudged along beside her.

"Come on, you've got to understand," Mary-Kate begged. "It's a Bulls game!"

And besides – I'm going for you, she thought.

"I know it's a Bulls game," Amanda complained. "You know I've been dying to go to one for weeks."

"I'm really sorry," Mary-Kate repeated. "What can I do? I promised Carrie, so I can't get out of it now."

"My mom's picking me up today," Amanda said. She veered off to the car without saying goodbye.

Oh, boy, Mary-Kate thought. *I've really hurt Amanda's feelings. But everything will be okay when she finds out about the surprise party. Then she'll thank me.*

I hope!

CHAPTER EIGHT

"He's definitely avoiding me," Ashley mumbled.

She and Mary-Kate stood in the hall during lunch the next day.

"Did you see that?" Ashley went on. "Parker was walking straight towards me. Then when he noticed me standing here by his locker, he turned around and went the other way!"

"Nah," Mary-Kate said. "He just changed his mind. He probably remembered he doesn't need his books next period."

Ashley shook her head. "No, he's avoiding me. I waited for him outside his French class yesterday. He acted like he didn't see me. And this morning I chased him all the way to the gym!"

"What happened?" Mary-Kate asked.

"He ducked into the boys' locker room and got away," Ashley answered.

"That never stopped you before!" Mary-Kate joked.

"Ha ha." Ashley shot a nervous glance at her sister. "You're not going to tell anyone that I don't have Parker locked in for my party, are you?"

"No way," Mary-Kate promised. "But tonight, when Toni Kukoc says he's coming to my party, I'm calling up everyone! I don't care how late it is!"

"That's fair," Ashley answered. She didn't think there was much chance Kukoc would come. "But the party's tomorrow. Everyone's already supposed to know which party they're going to."

"Uh-huh," Mary-Kate agreed. "But they could change their minds at the last minute."

Yes, they could, Ashley thought. *And they will – if they walk into my party, and Parker's not there!*

"We may as well go," Ashley said. "I'm sure Parker's not going to come back to his locker until I'm gone. You don't have any idea what class he has next, do you?"

"What class who has?" a voice behind Ashley asked.

Ashley whirled around. Jennifer was right behind her.

"Who are you talking about?" Jennifer asked.

"Don't tell me you've got a crush on someone new."

"A crush? On someone new? No way," Ashley said. "I was talking about Mr. Ramone. I have to see him about a make-up test."

"Oh," Jennifer said. "There he is now. You can ask him."

Ashley glanced over her shoulder. Mr. Ramone was coming down the hall.

"Uh, yeah. Great. I'll talk to him," Ashley said. "But maybe I'd better study for the test first. Bye!"

She rushed away, leaving Jennifer standing with Mary-Kate.

When she turned the corner, she saw Carly heading towards her. Ashley didn't want to hear Carly gush about how exciting it was going to be hanging out with Parker. She ducked into the bathroom.

Rebecca was perched on the bench near the sinks. She looked up and smiled. "Hey, Ashley. Do you have a minute? I'm doing the roving reporter column this month and I have to ask people what they would change about our school if they could."

"Friendlier guys," Ashley said.

"Good one," Rebecca answered. She wrote Ashley's answer down in a little notebook.

Ashley brushed her hair, then she figured it was probably safe to go back into the hall. Carly should be gone by now. And Jennifer, too.

She moved towards the door, and froze. Wait. Rebecca worked on the school newspaper. And so did Parker. Maybe Rebecca could help her out!

Ashley spun around. "Um, I have a friend who has a crush on Parker Branford. Any juicy titbits you can tell me about him?"

Like how to get him to my party, she added silently.

"I hope you're not talking about yourself," Rebecca answered. "If you are, you'll be disappointed. Parker's cute, but he's boring. He hasn't written a single word for the paper this year, because he can't think of anything. How lame is that?"

"Pretty lame," Ashley agreed. "But I'm not going to be able to convince my friend of that. So do you have any advice? He doesn't even seem to know she's alive."

Rebecca nodded. "He has a one-track mind," she said. "All he ever talks about is wanting to be a DJ."

A DJ. Like at a *party*. Score!

"Rebecca, you're the best!" Ashley cheered. She rushed over and gave her a hug.

"Tell your friend good luck," Rebecca said. "Although I think good luck might be getting over her crush on Parker."

"Probably. But she'll have to figure that out for

herself," Ashley agreed. "Hey, do you by any chance know where she might find Parker some time today?"

"I know he'll be in the journalism room after school," Rebecca answered. "We go to press tomorrow, so everyone will be there. Even the ones who haven't written anything!"

"Thanks," Ashley told her. "You have no idea how you just saved my, uh, my friend's life."

As soon as the last bell rang, Ashley jumped out of her chair and dashed out of class. She ran straight to the journalism room.

She took a quick peek inside. No Parker.

But he'd be there soon, and he wouldn't be able to avoid going right past her.

A few minutes later she saw Parker strolling down the hall. She knew the second he spotted her. His face got all tight, and his eyes narrowed into a squint.

"Hi!" Ashley called. She decided to pretend she didn't notice how unthrilled he was to see her.

Parker didn't try to avoid her this time. He walked right up and stopped about an inch away from her nose.

Ashley swallowed so hard, she figured everyone

in the whole school could hear.

"You're following me," Parker said. "And I want you to stop."

"No, no," Ashley stammered. "I'm not, not really. I'm . . . uh . . . I'm trying to hire you!"

"What?" Parker asked. He brushed his wavy hair out of his eyes. He looked at her as if she were nuts.

"Not for money or anything," Ashley explained quickly. "I was just wondering . . . Remember that party I told you about? Well, it's tomorrow night. Would you be willing to be the DJ?"

Parker's face lit up. "Seriously?" he asked.

Ashley nodded.

"Definitely!" he said. "On one condition. I get to pick all the music. I mean, I'm in charge – right?"

"No problem!" Ashley agreed as fast as she could. "Just remember: It's a surprise party for Jennifer. So don't say anything about it to her, okay?"

"Who?" he asked.

Ashley didn't care that he didn't have a clue who Jennifer was. He was coming to her party! And that meant everyone else was coming, too!

Unless Mary-Kate really did manage to talk to Toni Kukoc. But there was no way that could happen.

No possible way.

CHAPTER NINE

"Way to go, Kukoc!" Carrie screamed. "Hit that shot! Go Bulls!" She jumped up and down and waved her arms in the air. Mary-Kate jumped up and down right along with her.

It was the fourth quarter of the Bulls game. The Bulls were winning by two points. The players looked tiny from so high up in the arena. But Mary-Kate and Carrie were having a great time anyway.

"Two points! Yes!" Mary-Kate screamed. She grinned at Carrie. "After this game, Tony's going to be in such a great mood he'll say yes to anything."

At least I hope he does, she said to herself. She was beginning to feel nervous. Anything could go wrong.

What if I miss him? Mary-Kate thought. *What if I*

*lose my nerve? What if he says no? What if he says yes –
and doesn't come?*

Carrie put her hand on Mary-Kate's arm.
"Listen," she said. "I want to talk to you about Toni
Kukoc. You know he probably won't say he'll come
to the party. You'll be lucky to even get close to him
after the game. A lot of players hurry back to the
locker room and don't stop for anything. So, if this
doesn't work out . . ."

Mary-Kate shook her head. "Don't even think
that way!" she warned Carrie. "I'm talking to Toni.
That's the only reason I'm here! Then *he* can tell me
whether he can come or not!"

Carrie sighed and sat back in her seat. Mary-Kate
sat down next to her. They watched the rest of the
game without screaming.

Finally the Bulls called their last time-out. They
were ahead by six points. And there were only six
seconds left to play.

The group in front of Mary-Kate and Carrie
began to stand up and leave the arena.

"Hey, maybe we'd better go, too," Mary-Kate
said. "We've got to get down to the locker room
before the players get away."

Carrie nodded, and the two of them pushed
towards the steps.

But the steps were already filled with people. Zillions of them.

And every single one of them was taller than Mary-Kate.

"Could you please keep moving?" Mary-Kate pleaded with two guys in front of her. They had stopped and were staring at the scoreboard. No one could get past them.

One of the guys turned around and glared at Mary-Kate. "I can't move until the guy in front of me moves," he snapped. "And he can't move until the guy in front of him moves. Get it?"

"But there's empty space in front of you!" Mary-Kate protested.

The guy rolled his eyes. "Come on," he said to his friend. They moved up to the empty step ahead of them. And stopped.

Mary-Kate looked at Carrie. "We're not going anywhere," she moaned.

"Follow me," Carrie said.

She grabbed Mary-Kate and yanked her away from the steps. They hurried sideways, through an empty row of seats, towards the next stairway.

Then they raced down towards the court. But the crowd was almost as thick at the second level. Mary-Kate started to feel as if she couldn't breathe.

"Just hang in there a little longer," Carrie said. She kept her hand clasped around Mary-Kate's arm.

Finally they reached the first level. Mary-Kate spotted a tiny hole in the mob. She jerked away from Carrie, crouched down low, and ducked between the legs of a woman dressed all in Bulls' colours.

"Mary-Kate! Wait!" Carrie called. But Mary-Kate didn't listen. She dashed out on to the basketball court.

A security guard stepped in front of her, blocking her way. Mary-Kate leaped to the left. But the guard was fast. He blocked her again.

"No one's allowed on the court," he told her.

"But I have to get to the locker room," Mary-Kate insisted. "Toni Kukoc is my cousin. He said to meet him there after the game."

The guard shook his head. "It's amazing how many relatives Kukoc has. And how many girlfriends. And how many ex-babysitters. And how many old neighbours. And how many guys who went to high school with him."

"You don't believe me?" Mary-Kate exclaimed.

"Did Kukoc give you a pass?" the guard asked. "I believe everyone who shows me a pass."

Mary-Kate wasn't going to give up. Not now. Not when she was so close.

She patted the pockets of her jeans. She patted the pockets of her sweatshirt. She patted the pockets of her jeans again.

The guard shook his head again. "Please don't even try it," he said. "You know how many passes people claim to have lost in here? We should be buried in passes right now."

He took Mary-Kate gently by the shoulders and turned her around. "You can walk around the stadium and get to the outside locker-room door. Kukoc usually signs a few autographs on his way out. Maybe you'll get lucky."

Mary-Kate shot one last look at the locker room. She was so close to the *inside* door. But there was no way she'd be able to get by this guy.

She trudged back towards the crowd. Carrie snagged her the second she got close enough.

"We have to walk all the way around to the outside locker-room door," Mary-Kate said.

Carrie looked as if she wanted to tell Mary-Kate it was hopeless, but she just nodded. She curled her fingers around Mary-Kate's belt loop, and they dived back into the centre of the crowd.

When they finally burst outside, Mary-Kate

allowed herself three long breaths of the fresh air. Then she started to run around the stadium, with Carrie stumbling behind her.

"There's the door," she cried.

And there were the hundreds of other people waiting for autographs.

Mary-Kate gulped. "Well, I have to try," she said.

"You go ahead," Carrie suggested. "I'll wait for you here." She gave Mary Kate a thumbs up sign.

Mary-Kate plunged into the mass of people. Then she heard it. The crowd broke into a chant. "Ku-koc! Ku-koc! Ku-koc!"

Toni was coming out! But where was he? Mary-Kate stood on tiptoe, trying to see above the heads in front of her.

"Move back!" a guard shouted. He was trying to clear a path – right in front of Mary-Kate!

The crowd separated. Now Mary-Kate could see all the way to the door of the stadium.

Yes! There he was! Toni Kukoc was working his way along the line of people, smiling and signing autographs.

He came closer and closer. Mary-Kate tried to memorise what she would say to him. *Mr. Kukoc, would you please come to a birthday party for my friend Amanda?* she recited to herself. *She's your biggest fan and . . .*

"Yo, Tony!" the man next to her bellowed.

Mary-Kate blinked. Tony Kukoc was standing right in front of her! This was her big chance.

She craned her head up and tried to catch his eye. "Mr. Kukoc," she began rapidly. "Would you please come to a birthday party—"

"Hey, Toni, can I have your autograph?" a woman behind her interrupted. The woman thrust her arm in front of Mary-Kate and waved Toni Kukoc's photograph in the air. He reached out and signed it.

"The party's for my friend Amanda," Mary-Kate began again, even louder. "She's your biggest fan and—"

But Kukoc didn't even look down.

He took another step along the line. *He's going!* Mary-Kate thought. *I've got to do something.*

Quickly she pulled her programme out of her backpack and handed it to Kukoc. He scribbled his name and passed it back to her.

He gave her a big smile – and was gone.

"So what did he say?" Carrie asked when Mary-Kate made her way back through the crowd.

"You were right," Mary-Kate said. "There was no way Tony Kukoc was *ever* going to come to my party. But I did get his autograph." She showed

Carrie the programme with a big signature sprawled across it.

At least Mary-Kate would be able to give Amanda a great present.

But that wouldn't make up for a party with practically no guests!

CHAPTER TEN

"Dad? Where are the scissors?" Ashley called. "I've still got to wrap Jennifer's present!"

It was three o'clock on Saturday. The day of the party had finally arrived.

Kevin handed her the scissors. He had been using them to trim one of the silver streamers that hung down from the ceiling.

"Thanks," Ashley said. She cut the ribbon for the package and tied a bow.

Then she gazed at the living room. It was perfect. There were candles everywhere. And streamers looped up with lavender bows. And a couple of bouquets of real lavender roses that made the air smell as if it had been sprayed with perfume.

It was so elegant. She knew Jennifer would absolutely love it.

All the furniture had been pushed back so they could dance. And the food was ready. Fancy plastic glasses were lined up on a table near the wall.

Best of all, Ashley had bought the perfect dress. A shimmery blue satin slip-dress with spaghetti straps. It went perfectly with her silver and lavender colour scheme, naturally.

"Well, it looks like you're ready," Carrie said as she hurried into the room with another platter of pastries. She set the platter down, then did a slow turn so she could admire the room. "It's really lovely, Ashley."

"And the basement looks cool," she added as Mary-Kate joined them. "I'm not sure I'll be able to choose which party to hang out in!"

"Carrie!" Ashley screeched. "You promised."

Carrie laughed. "I know – just kidding. Your dad and I will hang out in the kitchen. Don't worry." She lowered her voice to a whisper. "I'll keep him busy refilling the dip bowls and stuff. We'll only make occasional appearances in the party rooms."

"You and Dad can come in the basement as much as you want," Mary-Kate said. "It's not as if anyone else is going to be there."

Mary-Kate wasn't absolutely sure how many people would be at her party. Rebecca and Carly never did make up their minds either way. And Max finally decided he wanted girls *and* anchovy and broccoli pizza. One thing she knew – there would definitely be more people at Ashley's party.

"I'm sure people from my party will go to yours, too. I mean, they're in the same house and everything," Ashley told her. "And no way I'm missing pin the tail. I'm not letting someone else take over my title as all-time champ."

"Thanks," Mary-Kate said. She brushed her hair off her face. "I think your party is going to be the best."

"Thanks," Ashley answered. She didn't know what else to say. She wanted to tell Mary-Kate just to forget about whose party was better, but she was afraid that would just make her sister feel worse.

Carrie glanced at her watch. "We've got two errands left," she reminded them. "You girls ready to go?"

Ashley nodded. She and Mary-Kate put on their coats, hats, gloves, and boots. A terrible storm had hit Chicago that day. The snow was two feet deep. And the roads were icy.

Kevin and Carrie bundled up, too. Then they got

into separate cars. Kevin and Mary-Kate were going for the birthday cakes. Carrie and Ashley were going to pick up the chocolate-covered strawberries.

"I hope your friends all get here on time," Carrie said as they drove. "The traffic is terrible because of the snow."

"Don't say that," Ashley said, a prickle of fear running down her spine. "I don't want a single thing to go wrong tonight. Not after everything I've gone through!"

"Oh, it won't," Carrie said quickly. "You've planned everything so carefully. You girls should be so proud. It'll be a night to remember forever, I'm sure."

She pulled up in front of the little candy shop and Ashley ran in and paid for the strawberries. She took a quick peek at them as she hurried back outside. They were beautiful, big and ripe, with long stems. The dark chocolate made the red of the berries look even richer.

Jennifer is going to fall on the floor when she sees these, Ashley thought. She climbed back into the car. She wished the time until the party would just disappear.

But when they arrived back at home, there were still two hours to go. Ashley rushed in from the cold. As she passed the answering machine, she saw the little red light flashing.

"We've got a message," she said. She pushed the button and continued on to the kitchen.

Until she heard who the message was from – Jennifer. Then she froze, listening hard.

"Hi, Ashley!" Jennifer said. She sounded happier than she had in weeks. "Guess what? You won't believe this, but I'm going to Disney World for my birthday!"

Ashley glanced at Carrie with a look of sheer panic. She almost dropped the strawberries, but Carrie grabbed them out of her hands.

"My parents just surprised me with the news," Jennifer went on. "Isn't that amazing? No wonder they wouldn't let me have a party this year! I'm such an idiot for sulking for two whole weeks – but who cares? We're all packed to go, and we're leaving in about two minutes. So, obviously, I can't come over to your house tonight to watch a video. Isn't that great? I'll send you a postcard! Wish me happy birthday. Bye!"

Ashley just stood there, staring at the answering machine. A huge lump formed in her throat.

Maybe her party plans were perfect, but what did it matter? Without Jennifer, Ashley's party was ruined!

CHAPTER ELEVEN

Mary-Kate took one glance at her sister and immediately knew that something bad had happened. "What's wrong?" she cried as she hurried over to Ashley.

"She's not home," Ashley moaned as she pressed the phone to her ear. "I've been calling for the past twenty minutes. No answer. They're gone!"

"Who's gone?" Kevin demanded.

"What's going on?" Mary-Kate cried. She knew it was something big.

Carrie quickly explained about the message on the answering machine, about how Jennifer was probably on a plane to Disney World right that second.

"You mean you didn't tell her parents about the surprise party?" Mary-Kate asked. Her eyes opened wide.

Ashley blushed. "I guess I forgot," she admitted. "I didn't even think that Mr. and Mrs. Dilber would have something planned. I thought they just didn't care about Jennifer's birthday. That's what Jennifer kept saying."

"Wow," Mary-Kate said. "I'm glad that's not going to happen to me. I sent Amanda's parents an e-mail and told them all about my party."

"How about a little more sympathy, Mary-Kate?" Carrie whispered.

"I'm sorry," Mary-Kate said. She wrapped her arm around Ashley's shoulders. "It just slipped out. I didn't mean to make you feel worse."

"It's okay. Nothing could make me feel worse," Ashley answered.

"Look," Carrie told Ashley. "Your guests will be here soon. They're expecting to have a good time – with or without Jennifer."

"And they will. Your party is going to be awesome, Ashley," Mary-Kate exclaimed, trying to make her voice super bright and cheery.

Ashley gave Mary-Kate a tiny smile. Mary-Kate smiled back. She knew how bad Ashley must be feeling right now. Mary-Kate's party might not have a lot of people, but it would have the guest of honour. And she and Amanda always had fun together.

The phone rang and Ashley answered it.

"Hello?" Ashley said. Then she covered the mouthpiece. "It's Amanda," she whispered to Mary-Kate. "But she doesn't sound happy."

"She will in a minute," Mary-Kate whispered back. "I'm going to invite her over now. I was waiting till the last minute."

She took the phone from Ashley.

"Hello?" Mary-Kate said.

"Mary-Kate?" Amanda said in a really angry voice. "I just want you to know that you're not my friend any more – and I never want to speak to you again as long as I live!"

"Amanda!" Mary-Kate gasped. "What's wrong?"

"Did you think I wouldn't find out?" Amanda yelled. "I know about your stupid parties! Parker Branford was going around telling everyone that you and Ashley are both having parties tonight. And you didn't invite me! I can't believe you'd treat a friend that way! And don't even bother calling me back, because I won't speak to you!"

Then she slammed the phone down in Mary-Kate's ear.

"What?" Ashley demanded. "What's going on?"

Mary-Kate didn't answer. She dialled Amanda's number as fast as she could.

Amanda answered on the first ring. "Hello?"

"Amanda, it's me. Please don't—"

SLAM!

Wow, Mary-Kate thought.

No one had ever been that mad at her before. Ever.

But she wasn't about to give up. She dialled Amanda's number again. This time Amanda's mother answered the phone.

"Amanda doesn't want to talk to you, Mary-Kate," Mrs. Bennett said in a cold voice. "She's really upset with you. Please don't keep calling. It's just making her feel worse."

"I don't believe this!" Mary-Kate said after Mrs. Bennett hung up. "Why is Mrs. Bennett mad at me? Doesn't she remember about the surprise party?"

"We went to all this trouble for nothing!" Ashley moaned.

Kevin glanced out of the window. "Well, not for nothing," he announced. "I see a car pulling up." Your guests are arriving."

Ashley raced to the window. "Oh, no," she cried. "It's Parker!"

68

She dashed into the bathroom to check her hair. Mary-Kate followed her. Ashley's hair was a mess after being out in the snow. But with a brush and some butterfly clips, she fixed it quickly. When she was done, it looked even better than it had before!

"Okay," Ashley announced, forcing a smile on to her face. "I'm having my party anyway – even if Jennifer isn't here!"

Ding-dong. The door bell rang.

Mary-Kate answered the door. Parker Branford was standing there – with a huge pile of equipment. He lugged two speakers, a turntable, and a bunch of cords into the house.

"Hi!" he said with a grin. "Dr. Cool, your DJ, has arrived."

Dr. Cool? Mary-Kate thought. *He calls himself Dr. Cool?*

Reality check!

Then she and Ashley caught a glimpse of his records. They were old vinyl records, not CDs.

Yikes! Mary-Kate thought when she saw the titles. Parker had brought the most uncool pile of music she'd ever seen!

"Tony Bennett?" Ashley blurted out. "Frank Sinatra? You like him?"

Parker shot her a glance. "Hey, it's retro. It's cool.

Like those khaki commercials with the swing dancing."

Ashley gulped. "Uh, right," she said. "Fine. Whatever. You're the DJ."

"That's right," Parker answered. "I *am* the DJ."

The doorbell rang again. More kids were arriving. And some of them were in jeans and sweaters. It looked like not everyone was a Parker Branford fan. Some people were coming to Mary-Kate's party, after all.

"This is the worst day of our lives," Ashley mumbled to Mary-Kate under her breath.

Not if I can help it, Mary-Kate thought.

She grabbed her coat and whispered in Carrie's ear. Then she turned to Ashley.

"Can you take care of both parties until I get back?" she asked.

"Sure," Ashley agreed. "Two disasters are no harder to handle than one. But where are you going?"

"Over to Amanda's," Mary-Kate announced. "I'm going to get her to this party, no matter what it takes!"

CHAPTER TWELVE

Mary-Kate sat shivering in Carrie's car. It was bitter cold outside. And the heater in Carrie's car had stopped working.

"Thanks for d-d-d-driving me to Amanda's," Mary-Kate stammered.

"Oh, no problem," Carrie answered. "I know how awful it is to be fighting with a friend. It's the worst."

Almost the worst, Mary-Kate thought. It wasn't quite as bad as fighting with Ashley.

"I just don't know why Amanda's mom was so mad on the phone," Mary-Kate muttered. "I mean, doesn't she remember I'm giving Amanda a surprise party tonight?"

Carrie gave Mary-Kate a sympathetic shake of the head. "Who knows?" she said.

She pulled up in front of Amanda's house. "I'll w-wait here," Carrie offered. Her teeth chattered. "Brrrrr. Good luck. And hurry!"

Mary-Kate went up to the back door and rang the bell. She peeked in through the window. Amanda was sitting at the kitchen counter. When she saw Mary-Kate peering in, she got up – and stormed off!

Wow, Mary-Kate thought. *She's not even going to answer the door!*

For a second Mary-Kate felt hurt. But then she got mad.

Amanda can't do this! she decided. *I'm having a surprise birthday party for her – whether she likes it or not!*

Mary-Kate tried the door handle. It was locked.

Then she glanced down and noticed the dog flap. It was a swinging rubber panel near the bottom of the regular door.

I'll bet I could get in through there! Mary-Kate thought. *But yuck. It's covered with dog slobber!*

Mary-Kate took a deep breath. Then she got down on her hands and knees. She pushed the dog flap open and crawled into Amanda's house.

Talk about the things you do for friendship!

When she stood up, she was in the Bennetts' kitchen.

Amanda stared at her from the hallway.

"I don't believe this!" Amanda cried. "Why won't you leave me alone?"

"Amanda, listen," Mary-Kate called. "I really want you to come to my party!"

"Sure," Amanda said. "*Now* you invite me! Look, I told you. I don't want to speak to you ever again. So get out!" She ran up the stairs to her bedroom.

Mary-Kate stood there, stunned.

A moment later Amanda's parents walked in from the family room. They both glared at her as if she was some kind of criminal.

"Mary-Kate, I'm not sure why you're here," Mrs. Bennett said.

Mary-Kate's eyes opened wide. "You aren't?" she said. Mary-Kate looked at Mr. and Mrs. Bennett. "Didn't you get my letter about the surprise party for Amanda?"

"Surprise party?" Mr. Bennett looked shocked. "No, we don't know anything about that!"

"But I sent you a long e-mail all about it!" Mary-Kate explained.

"An e-mail?" Mr. Bennett repeated. He turned to

Mrs. Bennett. "Have we checked the e-mail recently?"

"Not for weeks," Mrs. Bennett said, sounding as stunned as Amanda's father. "We really didn't know anything about a party."

"That explains it," Mary-Kate said. "I was planning to call Amanda half an hour ago and invite her to come over for a sleepover. There are already people at my house waiting to surprise her."

Amanda's parents both smiled. "E-mail is a great thing," Mr. Bennett said. "But maybe next time you plan a party, you could pick up the phone and tell us?"

"Hush," Amanda's mother said. She glanced towards the stairs. "We don't want to spoil the surprise now." She motioned for Mary-Kate to follow her to Amanda's room. "Come on. It's not too late. And by the way, Mary-Kate," she whispered. "I'm sorry. I should have known you'd never be mean to Amanda."

Mary-Kate felt the knot in her stomach loosen. Maybe it would all work out, after all.

"Amanda?" her mother called. She knocked on her daughter's door. "Can you please come out?"

Amanda opened the door. "What?" she snapped.

"Amanda, I really do want you to come to my party," Mary-Kate said. "I sent you an invitation – but you must not have got it."

"It probably got lost in the mail," Mrs. Bennett chimed in. "It was an honest mistake, Amanda. Don't you think you could forgive and forget?"

Amanda glared at her mother. "You're taking her side?" she complained.

"I'm just saying you two are friends, and you should try to make up," her mother said.

"No, thanks," Amanda answered. She went back in her room and slammed the door.

Mary-Kate glanced at her watch. It was almost 7:30. The party was probably in full swing!

Amanda's mother saw Mary-Kate looking at her watch.

"I don't know what to do," she whispered.

"Can't you make her come?" Mary-Kate whispered back.

Finally Mrs. Bennett opened Amanda's door and went in.

"Amanda," she said firmly, "Mary-Kate explained what happened. I think she deserves the benefit of the doubt. Now please put on your boots, get your coat, and go. I'm sure you'll have a great time."

Amanda's mouth dropped open. "I don't believe this!" she cried. "You're *making* me go to a party? That's so sick!"

But she grabbed her boots and shoved her feet

into them. In a huff she reached for her coat and followed Mary-Kate out to Carrie's car.

"I'm really glad you're coming," Mary-Kate said as they climbed in the back seat.

"I don't know why I'm bothering," Amanda snapped. "I'm going to have a terrible time."

"Oh, I don't know about that," Carrie commented. "Maybe you'll be surprised."

Mary-Kate turned her face to the side window so Amanda wouldn't see her smiling.

Surprised? Amanda was going to get the surprise of her life!

"Hey, look," Carrie said as they pulled up to the Burke house. "Isn't that Jennifer standing at the front door?"

"Yes!" Mary-Kate cried. She threw Carrie's car door open and leaped out. "Come on, Amanda. Let's catch up with her before she goes in!"

"Oh, great! Now you want to be with Jennifer more than with me?" Amanda complained.

"No, no," Mary-Kate said. She came back and took Amanda by the arm. "It's just that . . . that . . . Just, please, come on."

Mary-Kate hurried up to Jennifer, pulling Amanda behind her. "Hi! Hey, how come you're here? I thought you were going to Disney World."

Let's Party!

Jennifer turned around. Steam came out of her mouth in the cold. "Our flight was cancelled because of the snow," she said. "Can you believe it? My whole birthday is ruined!"

Suddenly Ashley threw open the front door. Inside, the house was filled with Amanda and Jennifer's friends. Balloons and streamers hung everywhere. And a huge banner stretched across the top of the doorway. It said: HAPPY BIRTHDAY JENNIFER AND AMANDA!

"Surprise!" everyone shouted at once. "Surprise!"

CHAPTER THIRTEEN

"Oh my gosh!" Amanda screamed. "Is this party really for . . . me?"

"*My* party is," Mary-Kate said. "Ashley's party is for Jennifer."

"Ashley!" Jennifer shrieked. She ran into Ashley's arms and gave her a huge hug.

"I don't believe this!" Amanda said. "Oh, Mary-Kate, I'm sorry! I acted like a complete jerk."

"That's okay. I probably would have done the same thing," Mary-Kate said quickly. "Come on. Your party is in the basement – I think!"

Mary-Kate glanced around the living room. Some of her friends were there at Ashley's party, already dancing.

For a minute she started to feel hurt. But then she saw two of the cutest guys Ashley had invited to her party. They were headed downstairs – to Mary-Kate's!

Mary-Kate caught Ashley's eye in the crowd.

"Everyone's just going to both parties!" Ashley shouted above the noise. "Isn't that great?"

"Yes!" Mary-Kate answered.

She looked around to see where Amanda was. To her amazement, Amanda was dancing! Someone had pulled her into the group, and she looked as if she was having a great time.

"Hey, Mary-Kate," Brian called out. "Check out this music. It's got to be fifty years old."

Everyone laughed – as if they thought Brian was making a joke.

But Mary-Kate sneaked a glance at the record jacket. The music was *more than* fifty years old!

When the song was over, Mary-Kate ran down to the basement and grabbed a handful of CDs. She carried them to Ashley and held them out.

"I know this is your party," she said. "So it's your call. But you can use my CD collection if you want."

"Do you really think I should?" Ashley asked. "I mean, what if Parker gets mad and leaves?"

"In my opinion," Mary-Kate said, "Parker's music has got to go – one way or the other!"

Ashley nodded. "I'd better check with Jennifer, though," she decided.

"Whatever," Mary-Kate said.

Mary-Kate made her way through the crowd, towards the basement.

Hip-hop music was blasting away downstairs.

"Mary-Kate, this party is awesome!" Michael Barnstein said.

He was sitting in front of a video game, madly working the controllers.

A bunch of other kids were playing Twister – on Carrie's bed! The mattress was squishy, so everyone kept falling down. Playing on the bed made it even funnier!

Mary-Kate spotted Nicole and Akilah tangled up with the others.

They were invited to Ashley's party! Mary-Kate thought. *And they were all dressed up for it.*

So what are they doing down here? she wondered.

Then she spotted Trevor Domingo, Parker's best friend. He was in the Twister group, too.

That explains it, Mary-Kate decided. He must have come to hang out with Parker. And since Nicole had a major crush on him, she followed him downstairs.

Hey – that's cool with me, Mary-Kate thought.

Everyone is *going to both parties!*

A few minutes later Amanda came downstairs. "I'm having so much fun!" she said. "Thank you, Mary-Kate. This is the best night of my whole life!"

Mary-Kate beamed. She couldn't be happier herself. Everything had worked out just the way she planned.

Well, almost everything, she thought.

Okay, face it. Nothing had turned out exactly the way she planned it. But it didn't matter. The party was awesome, anyway!

When it was time for birthday presents, everyone gathered in the living room. Amanda opened hers first.

"Toni Kukoc's autograph!" she squealed.

"Well, it was supposed to be Toni Kukoc himself," Mary-Kate admitted. "But I couldn't get him to come."

"Well, of course not," Amanda said. She beamed at Mary-Kate. "But that's okay. I get to keep his autograph forever!"

Everyone laughed.

For the next forty minutes, Jennifer and Amanda opened presents from all the guests.

Then it was time for cake.

Then more dancing and games.

Finally everyone went home – after telling Mary-Kate and Ashley that it was the best party they'd ever been to in their lives.

Mary-Kate and Ashley were exhausted as they climbed the stairs to bed.

"Whatever happened with Jennifer and Parker?" Mary-Kate asked. "I mean, I saw him hanging around. Even after you made him stop playing those records."

"He stayed for the food," Ashley admitted. "What a pig! He ate almost half of the chocolate-covered strawberries himself!"

Mary-Kate put on her PJs. "Did Jennifer get to dance with Parker?" she asked.

Ashley shook her head. "She followed him around for half the night. But then she realised he's totally boring! All he did was eat! Now she has a crush on Trevor Domingo."

"Uh-oh," Mary-Kate said. "What about Nicole? I thought she liked him."

Ashley slipped into her nightgown.

"Oh, that was yesterday," Ashley chided her. "Nicole likes Michael Barnstein now. You've got to stay awake if you want to keep up with everything!"

Stay awake? Mary-Kate thought. *No way!*

She was so sleepy, she could hardly keep her eyes open.

But she was happy, too. This had been the best party ever. It was so much better than it would have been without Ashley and all her friends, Mary-Kate realised.

"Good night, girls," her father called out. He stuck his head in the doorway. "Congratulations on a successful party. Amanda and Jennifer were really surprised. And tomorrow – I have a really big surprise for both of you!"

"Huh?" Mary-Kate said, startled.

But Kevin had already left and closed the door behind him.

"What do you think he means, Ashley?" Mary-Kate asked.

Ashley snored.

She's already asleep, Mary-Kate realised. *Oh, well. We'll have to wait till tomorrow to find out.*

CHAPTER FOURTEEN

Ashley rubbed her eyes and stumbled down the stairs for breakfast. Mary-Kate was right behind her.

"Hi, Dad," Ashley mumbled sleepily. Then she glanced around the living room in shock. "Whoa! What happened here?"

The night before, when Mary-Kate and Ashley went to bed, the living room was a huge mess. Streamers, plastic cups, and popped balloons were strewn all over the floor.

But now everything was completely neat. There wasn't a speck of dust anywhere.

"I thought *we* were supposed to clean up," Ashley said.

"Yeah," Mary-Kate chimed in. "You said it

would take us all day. Is this the surprise you were talking about?"

Kevin smiled mysteriously. "No, that's a different surprise. Let's have some breakfast, and I'll tell you about it."

Ashley glanced at the dining table. Carrie had set out a special breakfast. The smell of freshly baked blueberry muffins filled the air.

Ashley raised an eyebrow. "What's up, Dad?" she asked.

"First have a seat," he said.

The two girls sat down at the table. Mary-Kate picked up a blueberry muffin and took a bite. But Ashley couldn't eat.

Not until she found out what the mystery was all about!

Kevin and Carrie sat opposite the girls.

"Well," Kevin began slowly. "I don't know where to begin."

"Anywhere will do," Mary-Kate said. "Just so you get to the punch line."

"Okay," Kevin said, "here it is. You remember we talked about your going to boarding school?"

Ashley nodded. "Sure. White Oak Academy for Girls. That place we visited in New Hampshire last summer. It was really pretty. I loved the ivy-covered buildings."

"That's great – because they've accepted your applications," Kevin said. "You and Mary-Kate are officially in."

"Yeah!" Mary-Kate cheered. "I'd love to live in a dorm – with no parents around." She grinned. "So, we're off to boarding school next autumn?"

"Well, not exactly," Kevin said. "You know that rainforest expedition I applied to go on – the one to South America?"

The girls nodded.

"It came through," Kevin said. "I'm all set to go to Brazil."

"Way to go, Dad," Ashley exclaimed.

"That's awesome!" Mary-Kate said. "Does that mean Ashley and I will have the house to ourselves next summer?" She turned to Carrie. "You'll stay with us, won't you? We'll have a blast!"

"Um, I don't think I'll be able to," Carrie admitted. She looked at Kevin.

"Actually, the expedition starts this January," Kevin explained. "Right after Christmas vacation. And Carrie is coming with me, as an assistant."

Ashley's mouth dropped open. "What's going to happen to us?"

"Can we come too?" Mary-Kate asked. "I've

always wanted to see a real live jungle."

Ashley grimaced. "With real live snakes and tarantulas. I don't think so."

"No jungle for you this year," Kevin said. "As of January fifth, you will begin your first term at White Oak Academy!"

"What?" Mary-Kate almost choked on her muffin.

Wow, Ashley thought. *We'll be going away – so soon? This is unbelievable!*

Ashley glanced at her sister. Mary-Kate's face had turned as white as paper.

"But we were going to go to White Oak next autumn, not now," Mary-Kate objected. "I'm not ready to go yet."

"You've already been there to visit," Kevin pointed out. "So it won't be completely unfamiliar. And your cousin Jeremy will be right down the road, at the Harrington School for Boys."

A boys' school right down the road? Ashley thought about it for less than a minute. A whole school full of new, cute boys?

"Cool!" she shrieked.

"It's not cool," Mary-Kate complained. She dropped the rest of her muffin on her plate, "I can't go to boarding school this spring, and that's final."

Then she stood up and went into the living room.

"Maybe I should go talk to her," Carrie offered.

Ashley shook her head. "No. Let me. I know how she feels."

Ashley ran into the living room and found her sister Mary-Kate sitting on the sofa.

"Mary-Kate," Ashley said softly, "we'll make new friends at White Oak. Things will be great – I'm sure of it."

Mary-Kate folded her arms and gazed at her sister. "That's not the problem," she said with a sigh. "I know we'll make new friends, but spring is *softball* season. I've got to stay here in Chicago. I'm supposed to be starting pitcher for the team."

So that's it, Ashley thought. She remembered how much fun Mary-Kate had last year playing softball. She was one of the stars of the team. Ashley could see why Mary-Kate wouldn't want to leave all that behind.

"But you can always play softball at White Oak Academy," Ashley argued. "I'll bet they have a great team there."

"No way," Mary-Kate shook her head firmly. "How am I supposed to just walk out on all my teammates and friends? We have a chance for the championship this year! If I leave, I'll be letting them down."

"Just tell them you don't have any choice,"

Ashley suggested. "Tell them your dad is making you go."

"That's not completely true," a voice said behind her.

Ashley whirled around. Her dad stood in the doorway, looking serious.

"I'm not forcing you to go," Kevin said. "You girls do have another choice."

"What?" Mary-Kate asked eagerly.

"Well, I suppose you could move in with Mrs. Baker down the street. She could babysit for you girls while I'm gone," Kevin offered.

Mrs. Baker? Ashley thought. *What a terrible idea!* Mrs. Baker was nice – as a neighbour. But she was too old-fashioned. And she didn't understand kids very well.

Ashley exchanged glances with Mary-Kate.

"No way," they both said. "We'll go to White Oak!"

Mary-Kate sighed. "I guess the softball team will just have to make it on their own this year." She grinned. "And who knows – maybe they'll win without me!"

Kevin crossed the room and gave her a hug. "Good," he said. "I know you'll love it there. And you'll have your cousin Jeremy to show you the ropes. Now," Kevin said excitedly, "I have one more surprise for you."

"Another surprise?" Mary-Kate laughed. "I don't know if I can take any more surprises!"

Ashley noticed that her father was holding something behind his back. She felt her stomach do a little flip-flop. What was it now?

"You know I'm really going to miss you girls," Kevin said with a sad note in his voice. "This will be the first time we've been apart for more than a few days. But this rainforest trip is a once-in-a-lifetime chance for me. I just couldn't pass it up."

"I know, Dad," Mary-Kate said. "We know you're not trying to dump us, or anything."

"What's the surprise?" Ashley demanded. She could hardly wait.

"Here," Kevin said. He brought out two beautiful velvet-covered diaries from behind his back. "One for each of you. So that while we're apart, you can write down all your new experiences. Your thoughts and dreams. That way, when I get back, I can read all about everything that's happened to you."

He handed a plum-coloured diary to Ashley, and a deep blue one to Mary-Kate.

Ashley glanced at her diary, then shot a quick

look at her sister.

"Uh, great, Dad," Mary-Kate said. "But uh . . . what if . . ."

"Oh, don't worry," Kevin added quickly. "If there's something you don't want me to know about, that's fine. Just fold back the page and I won't read it. I'll know that part is private."

Ashley beamed and hugged the diary close to her.

"Okay," she said. "Thanks."

"Well, I'll let you girls start thinking about what to take to school with you," he said as he headed back downstairs.

Mary-Kate plopped down on her bed again. "I can't believe this is happening!" she said. "Moving to a new school in just a few weeks! I wonder what it'll be like. Do you think we'll be in the same dorm room?"

"Who knows," Ashley said. Her mind raced with a million questions. "I wonder if we'll have to wear uniforms?"

"Will the other girls be snotty or nice?" Mary-Kate chimed in.

Ashley grinned. "And will all the cute guys at the Harrington School already have girlfriends?"

"I guess we'll just have to wait until January to find out," Mary-Kate said. "You know, Ashley, this really *is* exciting."

"It's the most exciting thing that's ever happened to us," Ashley agreed.

Going to White Oak is the beginning of an adventure, she thought. *Who knows what the next few months will bring?*

But Ashley knew one thing. She'd have a lot to write in her diary every single day!

You won't believe it!

Mary-Kate and Ashley are off to boarding school.
Follow them to White Oak Academy in the

Two of a Kind™ Diaries

Super
Special ❶

Calling All Boys

Monday

Dear Diary,
News flash: Mary-Kate and I will not be sharing a
room here at the White Oak Academy!!

White Oak
Academy

"Twins never share a room," Mrs. Pritchard, the
headmistress, told us today. "It's all part of White
Oak tradition."

In case you haven't already noticed, Diary,

tradition rules at White Oak. But then Mrs. Pritchard told us the reason for the split. "We want twins to develop their own interests and make new friends."

Sure, it made sense. But knowing that Mary-Kate would be all the way down some hall made it even harder to say goodbye to Dad. I feel like I'm losing my family!

Dad left this afternoon, right after we met Mrs. Pritchard. "Okay, girls," Dad said. He took a long, deep breath. "I guess this is it." He held out his arms and gave each of us a big hug.

"Bye, Dad," I sniffed as he took a few steps back. "Have fun saving the Amazon rainforest."

"Yeah," Mary-Kate said. "And send us a parrot. So he can repeat everything Ashley says when I'm not around."

Very funny!

"Oh, which reminds me," Dad said. He reached into his black briefcase. "I brought a little present for both of you. Something that will come in handy."

And right before our very eyes Dad pulled out - are you ready, Diary? - a tiny black mobile phone! I couldn't believe it!! The only kid I know with a mobile is Jennifer Dilber. She uses her mobile so much that - well, you've heard of hat

hair? Jennifer has phone
hair!

"Are you sure this is for
us?" Mary-Kate asked.

"Sure I'm sure," Dad said.
He handed the phone to me.
"Unless you know any other
twins who are going away to
school for four whole
months."

Jennifer
with
phone
hair

There was no time to waste. I began punching in
Jennifer's number. I mean, I had to tell someone the
good news, right?

Wrong! Dad told us in his most serious Dad-
voice that the phone is to be used for emergencies
only. Bummer.

"I'll be carrying my phone wherever I go so you
can reach me any time," Dad explained.

Tarzan Dad

The thought of Dad having
a mobile in the jungle blew me
away. I mean, Tarzan should
be so cool!

Then the fun was over
and it was really time for
Dad to leave. As he walked
down the hall, Mary-Kate and I waved goodbye. We
were still waving after Dad left the building.

"Hello, Mary-Kate, hello, Ashley," a voice said.

Mary-Kate and I whirled around. A woman with blonde hair stood behind us.

"I'm Miss Viola, the dorm housemother," she explained. "Now, would you like to meet your roommates?" she asked us. "I'm sure they want to meet you!"

I felt a shiver of excitement. My new life at the White Oak Academy for Girls was about to begin!

Miss Viola brought me to my room first: Number 25 on the third floor. Room 25. It had a nice ring to it.

"I'm in Room Twenty-five," I practised saying inside my head. "You know. The one with all the pizza parties and late-night chats?"

After saying goodbye to Mary-Kate and wishing her luck, I grabbed the handle and opened the door.

"Hello?" I said, stepping inside. "Anybody home?"

No one answered. I looked around the room. The windows had strings of beads instead of curtains. One bed was covered with an Indian print bedspread and a pile of pillows.

There were posters on the walls, but not of celebrities - they were of William Shakespeare and this depressed-looking lady with her hair in a bun!

"Where am I?" I whispered to myself.

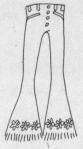

Depressed-looking lady (not Phoebe)

A girl with curly hair and blue-rimmed glasses peeked out from behind a wicker screen. "Hi," she said in a small voice. "I'm Phoebe Cahill. I guess we're roommates."

"I'm Ashley Burke." I walked around the screen to shake Phoebe's hand. She was sitting at a desk reading a book. I could see the title on the cover: Romeo and Juliet!

"Romeo and Juliet!" I sighed. "Did you see the movie with Claire Danes and Leonardo DiCaprio? It was awesome!"

Phoebe blinked a couple of times behind her glasses. "If you say so," she said with a little shrug.

I sat down on my unmade bed and waited for my trunk to arrive. Phoebe didn't seem like the chatty type, so I tried to break the ice. Chip by chip.

"I hope there's a decent mall around here," I said. Clothes are always a good icebreaker, right? Wrong!

"Oh, I don't shop at malls," Phoebe said. "I buy all my clothes at vintage shops."

Phoebe jumped up, ran to our closet, and started

pulling things out. She held up a pair of bell-bottom jeans.

"These jeans are from 1970!" Phoebe said excitedly. Then she picked up a pair of brown suede hip boots. "And these were worn by a real 1960s flower child!"

"I have a lava lamp at home," I said, trying to be cool. "It belonged to a real '70s disco king. My dad."

Phoebe looked bored when I started talking about my friends and my favourite rock groups. She actually thought 'N Sync was a drain cleaner!

This is Phoebe

"I really should go back to my book," Phoebe said politely. "Romeo was about to take the poison."

"Sure," I said as Phoebe slipped back behind the screen. "I'll be really quiet. Like a mouse."

I lay back on my bed and stared at the ceiling.

Okay, Phoebe Cahill is nice, even though she's not exactly what I expected.

But I guess there'll be lots of surprises for me and Mary-Kate from now on!

Tuesday

Dear Diary,
   I did it!!! I didn't think I could, but I, Mary-Kate Burke,
survived my first night at the White Oak Academy
for Girls.

Dad, wait up!

                              The first few hours
                              weren't easy. When I
                              heard that Ashley and I
                              weren't going to be
                              roommates, I felt like
                              chasing Dad all the way
                              to the Amazon - snakes
or no snakes. But when I stepped into Room
33 on the third floor, I knew things were
going to be cool.
   Why the sudden change? Picture this...
   The first thing I saw were shelves full of
sports trophies! And posters on the walls
of Derek Jeter and Sammy Sosa.
   Was I in my new room - or in heaven?
   Then my roommate Campbell Smith
walked in. She has short brown hair and
green eyes. And I knew she was an athlete by the way
she shook my hand - a real bone-crusher!
   Here comes the real kick - Campbell told me she was

my new roomie

the pitcher for the middle-grade softball team, the Mighty Oaks!!! She told me that maybe I could play on their team.

Hmm, I thought. Maybe the White Oak Academy for Girls won't be so bad after all!

But I did miss Ashley last night. It was weird having a strange girl sleeping in the next bed. Especially when she snores like a buzz saw!

That's why it was so neat to see Ashley first thing at Morning Announcements. That's when everyone piles into the auditorium to yawn and
listen to what Mrs. Pritchard has to tell us. As for me – I couldn't stop thinking about breakfast!

"What's that noise?" Ashley whispered to me.

"My stomach is growling," I said, grabbing my middle. "It probably misses our late-night snacks back in Chicago."

"I miss them, too," Ashley sighed. "The peanut-butter-and-marshmallow sandwiches, crisps with ketchup dip—"

"—milk with maple syrup," I added.

Diary, the food here is pretty decent but it's going to take a while to get used to eating in school all the time. And last night at dinner I made the mistake of calling the room we ate in "the cafeteria". Boy, did everyone get a kick out of that!

"It's the dining hall!" our new friend Wendy said.

"The dining hall!" I repeated in my most posh voice.
Wendy had a point. That room didn't look like any
school cafeteria I'd ever seen. The floors were made of
dark polished wood. So were the walls,
which were covered with old portraits
of women. Ashley guessed they were
past headmistresses. As for the gargoyles on the ceiling,
they're way cool. Even though they looked
like they were about to swoop down any
minute and grab our fried chicken!

Back in the auditorium, my stomach piped
down just as Mrs. Pritchard walked onto
the stage.

hungry gargoyles

"Good morning, girls," Mrs. Pritchard
said. "Why don't we start the day by greeting our two
newest White Oak girls, Mary-Kate and Ashley
Burke?"

Ashley jumped up and started waving to
everyone like a movie star. I just nodded and
cracked a smile.

After talking about the new school computer and gym suits, Mrs. Pritchard looked
really excited. "Girls, February is right around
the corner, and you know what that means!"
she said with a sly smile. "Next week is our

Ashley waving
at her
fans

annual Sadie Hawkins Day dance with the Harrington School for Boys!"

Mrs. P. gave us all a few seconds to whisper and get excited. Ashley looked pretty excited herself.

"A dance?" Ashley gasped. "You mean with a DJ?"

A girl in front of us turned around. "It's a square dance," she whispered. "You know - do-si-do and swing your partner - that kind of stuff."

"A square dance?" Ashley groaned. "Cor-ny!"

Corn Dancing

But then Mrs. Pritchard said the magic words.

"As you know," she said, "the Sadie Hawkins Day Dance is the only event where the girls must ask out the boys."

Everyone let out this earsplitting cheer.

"Now that's my kind of square dance!" Ashley said. She pumped her fist in the air. "Bring on the fiddles!"

The Sadie Hawkins Day Dance sounded like fun. But there was one problem. A major problem...

"Ashley?" I whispered. "I don't want to burst your bubble. But how are we going to ask out boys...when we don't know any?"

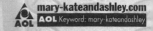

mary-kateandashley

TWO of a kind ™

Coming soon – can you collect them all?

HarperCollins*Entertainment*

PARACHUTE PRESS

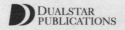
DUALSTAR PUBLICATIONS

mary-kateandashley.com
AOL Keyword: mary-kateandashley

mary-kateandashley

Meet Chloe and Riley Carlson.
So much to do...

so little time

(1)	How to Train a Boy	(0 00 714458 X)
(2)	Instant Boyfriend	(0 00 714448 2)
(3)	Too Good to be True	(0 00 714449 0)
(4)	Just Between Us	(0 00 714450 4)
(5)	Tell Me About It	(0 00 714451 2)
(6)	Secret Crush	(0 00 714452 0)

... and more
to come!

HarperCollins*Entertainment*

 PARACHUTE PRESS

 DUALSTAR PUBLICATIONS

 **mary-kateandashley.com**
AOL Keyword: mary-kateandashley

Mary-Kate and Ashley in their latest movie adventure

Available on video from 11th March

mary-kateandashley.com
AOL Keyword: mary-kateandashley

DUALSTAR VIDEO

Get ready to celebrate with the

Real Dolls for Real Girls

Mary-Kate & Ashley *Birthday Bash*

Fashion Dolls!

Celebrate with birth-
day cake, present, and
a camera to capture
the memories!

Plus a hip floral halter
dress included for
trendy birthday style!

DUALSTAR CONSUMER PRODUCTS

mary-kateandashley

mary-kateandashley.com
AOL Keyword: mary-kateandashley

MATTEL

Order Form

To order direct from the publishers, just make a list of the titles you want and fill in the form below:

Name ....

Address ....

....

....

Send to: Dept 6, HarperCollins Publishers Ltd, Westerhill Road, Bishopbriggs, Glasgow G64 2QT.

Please enclose a cheque or postal order to the value of the cover price, plus:

UK & BFPO: Add £1.00 for the first book, and 25p per copy for each additional book ordered.

Overseas and Eire: Add £2.95 service charge. Books will be sent by surface mail but quotes for airmail despatch will be given on request.

A 24-hour telephone ordering service is available to holders of Visa, MasterCard, Amex or Switch cards on 0141- 772 2281.

Collins
An *Imprint* of HarperCollins*Publishers*